DATE DUE

GAYLORD | | | PRINTED IN U.S.A.

I FEEL A FOOT!

Text copyright © 2008 by Maranke Rinck
Illustrations copyright © 2008 by Martijn van der Linden

Originally published in the Netherlands by Lemniscaat b.v. Rotterdam, 2008,
under the title **Ik voel een voet!**
All rights reserved
Printed in Belgium
First U.S. edition, 2008

CIP data is available

Lemniscaat
An Imprint of Boyds Mills Press, Inc.
815 Church Street
Honesdale, Pennsylvania 18431

Maranke Rinck &
Martijn van der Linden

I Feel a Foot!

Lemniscaat
Honesdale, Pennsylvania

Between two trees, hanging high above the grass, Turtle, Bat, Octopus, Bird, and Goat are asleep in their hammock.

Suddenly, Turtle opens his eyes. "Hey," he whispers, "do you hear what I hear?"

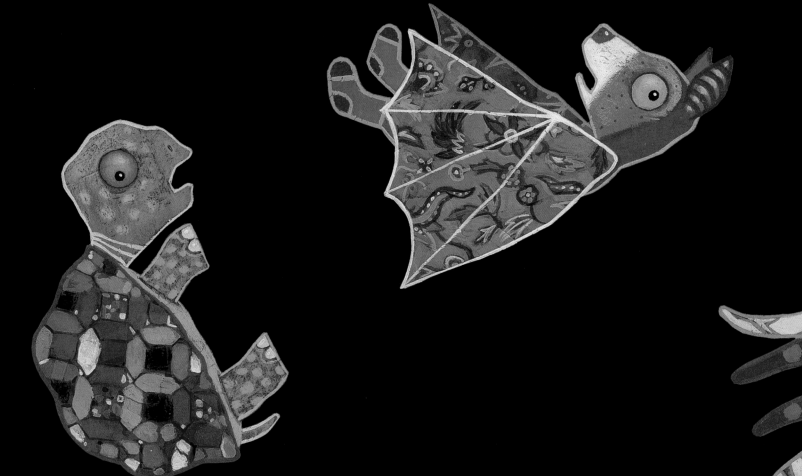

It's pitch dark. There's no moon. And not a star in the sky.
"Hey," whispers Turtle again.
Now the others are awake. They try to sit up. The hammock
starts to swing.

"Careful!" yells Turtle.
"We're tipping over!"
But it's too late.

"Shh," whispers Turtle. "Listen!"
"There's something in the field," whispers Bat.
"Something rustling," yawns Octopus.
"Heeelp!" cheeps Bird.
"Come on," whispers Goat. "On tiptoe!
And stick together! Let's investigate."

They sneak through the fields.

"Halt," whispers Goat. "Stop here, or we might bump into it, whatever it is. Don't move a muscle. And listen!"

"Goat," Turtle whispers after a while, "this investigation is getting us nowhere. I'm going to see what I can feel."

"I felt a foot!" Turtle says, running back. "Just like **my** foot—but super big. A super big turtle is rustling around out there!"

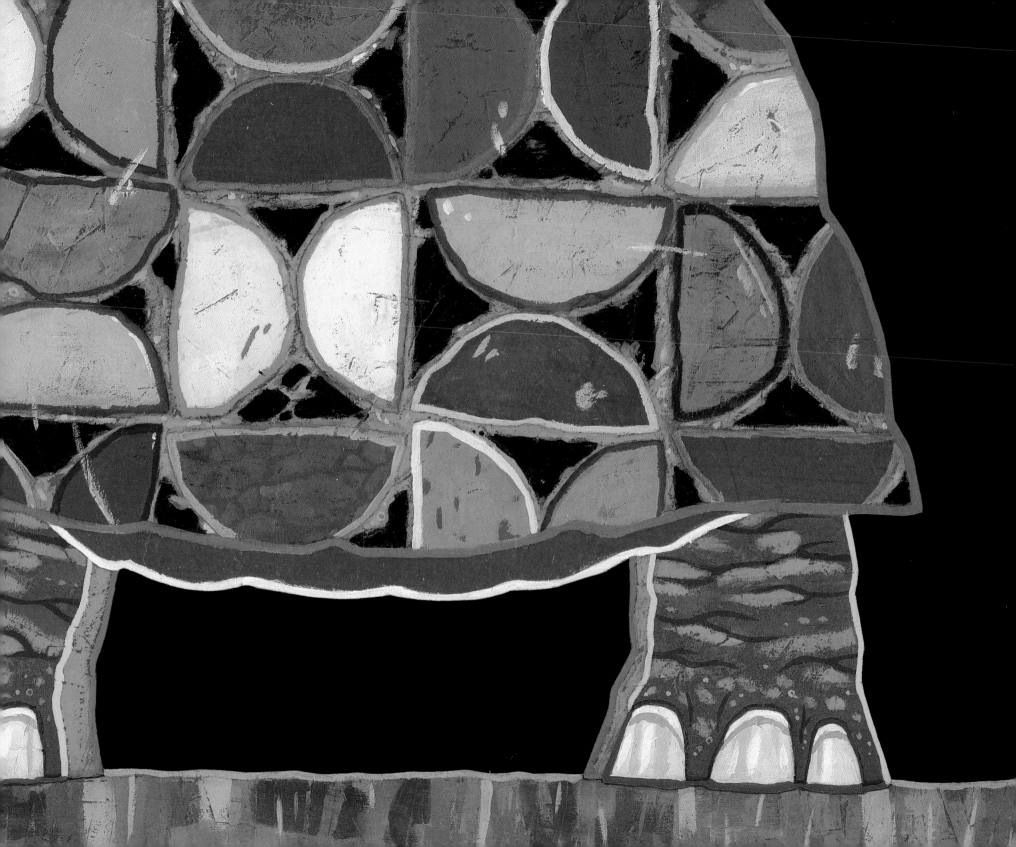

"A super big turtle?" Bat flaps her wings.
"Really?" Up she goes. "This I've got to see."

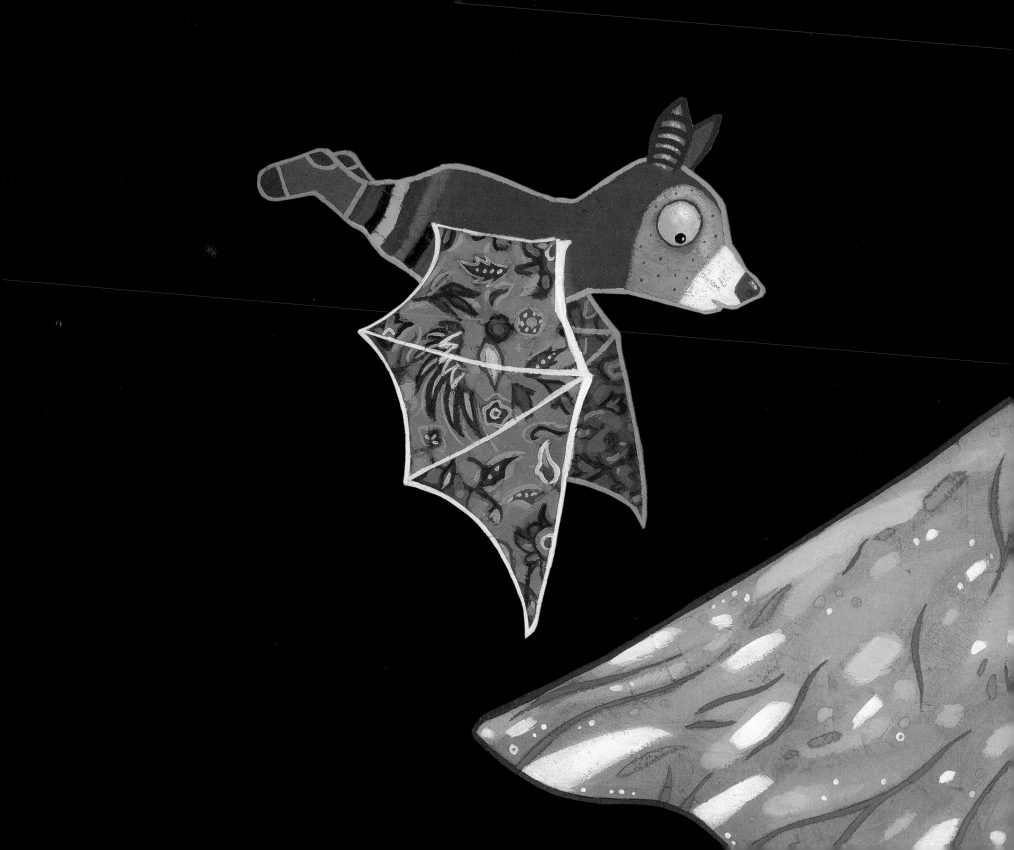

"I felt a wing," Bat whispers. "Just like **my** wing—but superduper big. A superduper big bat is rustling out there!"

"How confusing," whispers Octopus.
"What is it, a turtle or a bat?"
She creeps up cautiously.

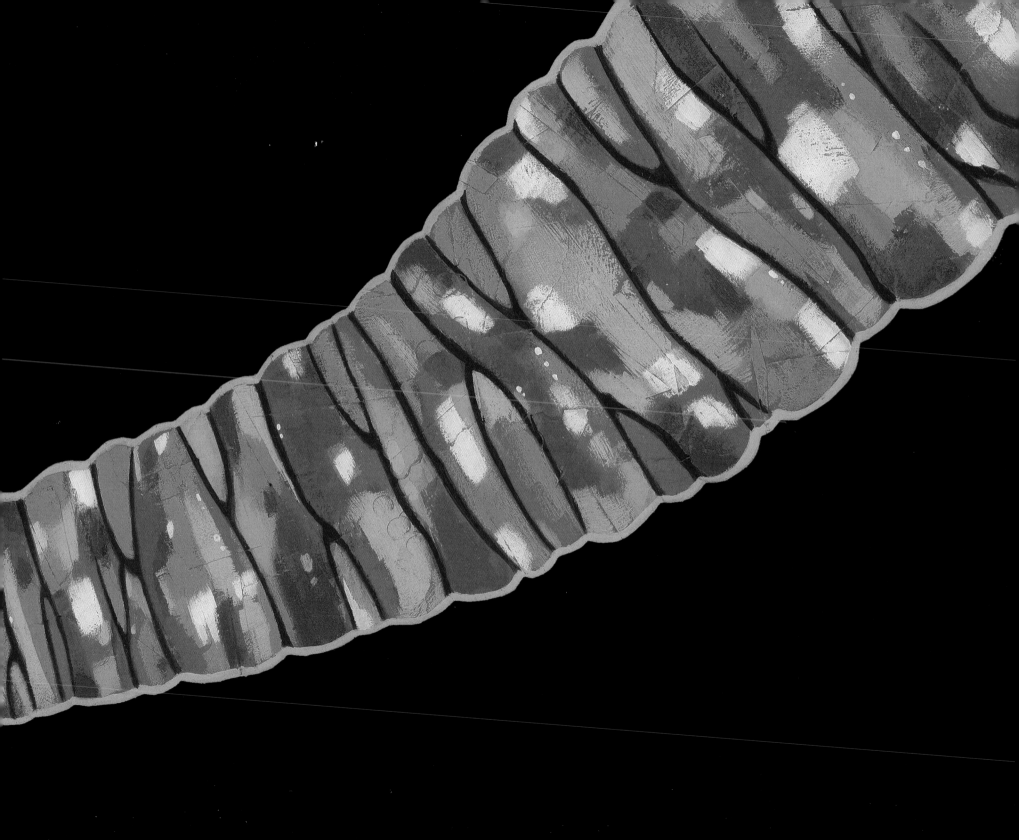

"That's not a turtle or a bat!" Octopus whispers excitedly.
"I felt a tentacle. Just like **my** tentacles—
but extra superduper big. An extra superduper
big octopus is rustling out there!"

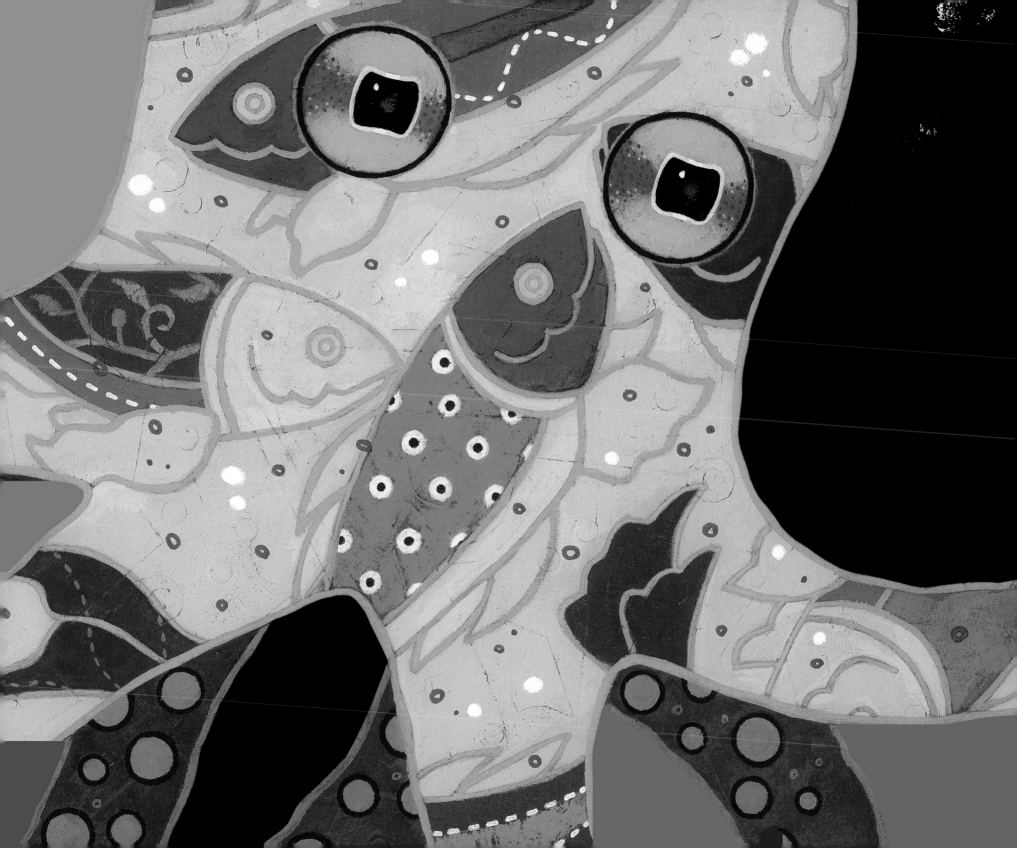

"Oy-oy-oy," Bird chirps. "Should I go, too?
I'm not really scared. Well, maybe just a little.
Should I? Very carefully?"

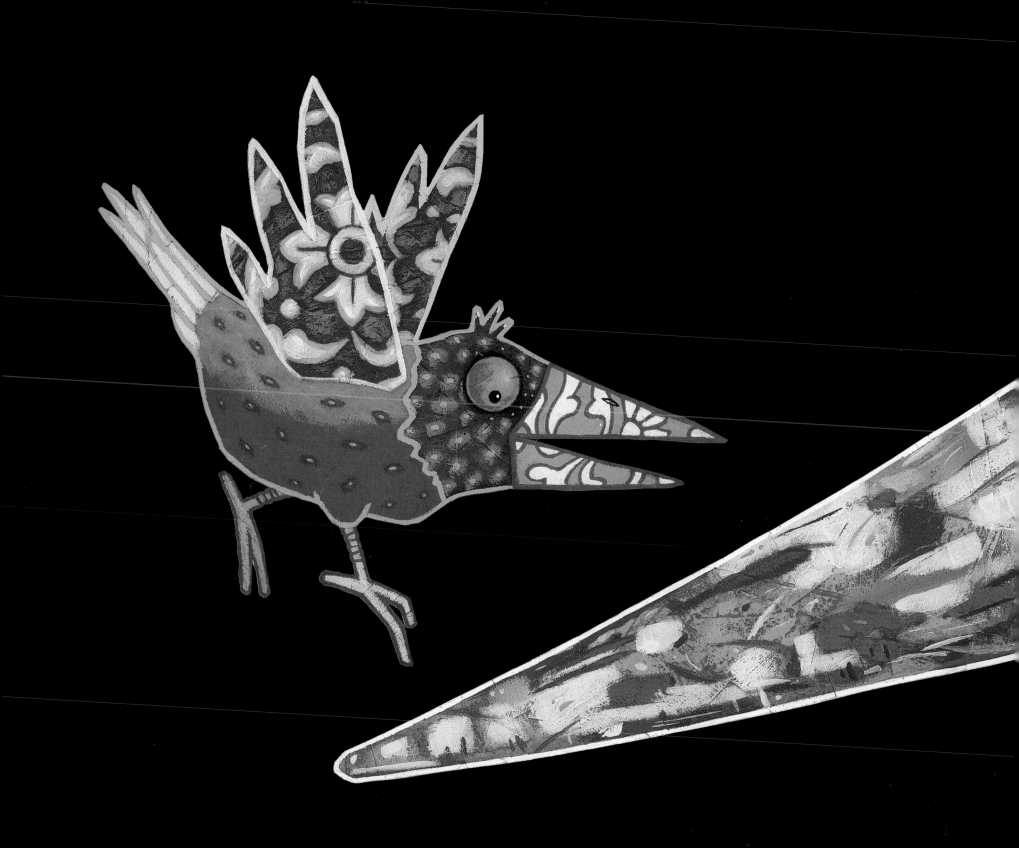

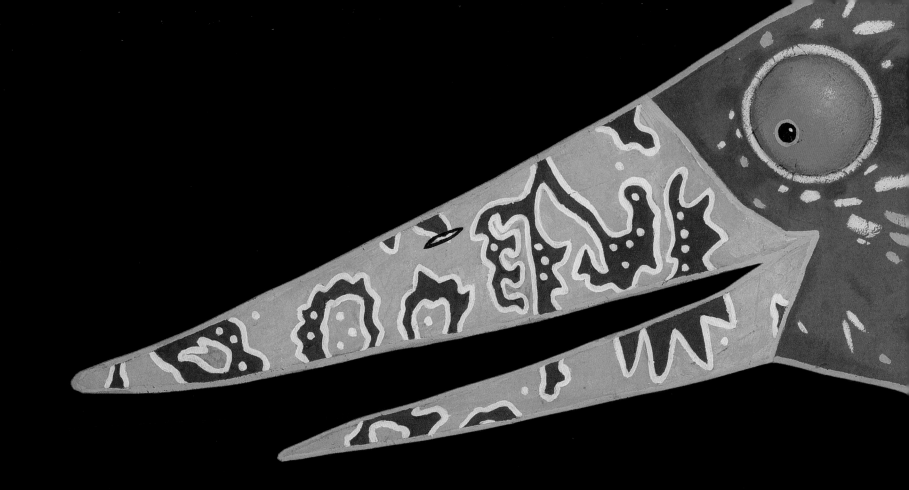

"Heeelp!" Bird whispers a minute later. "I felt a beak. Just like **my** beak—but amazingly extra superduper big. An amazingly extra superduper big bird is out there!"

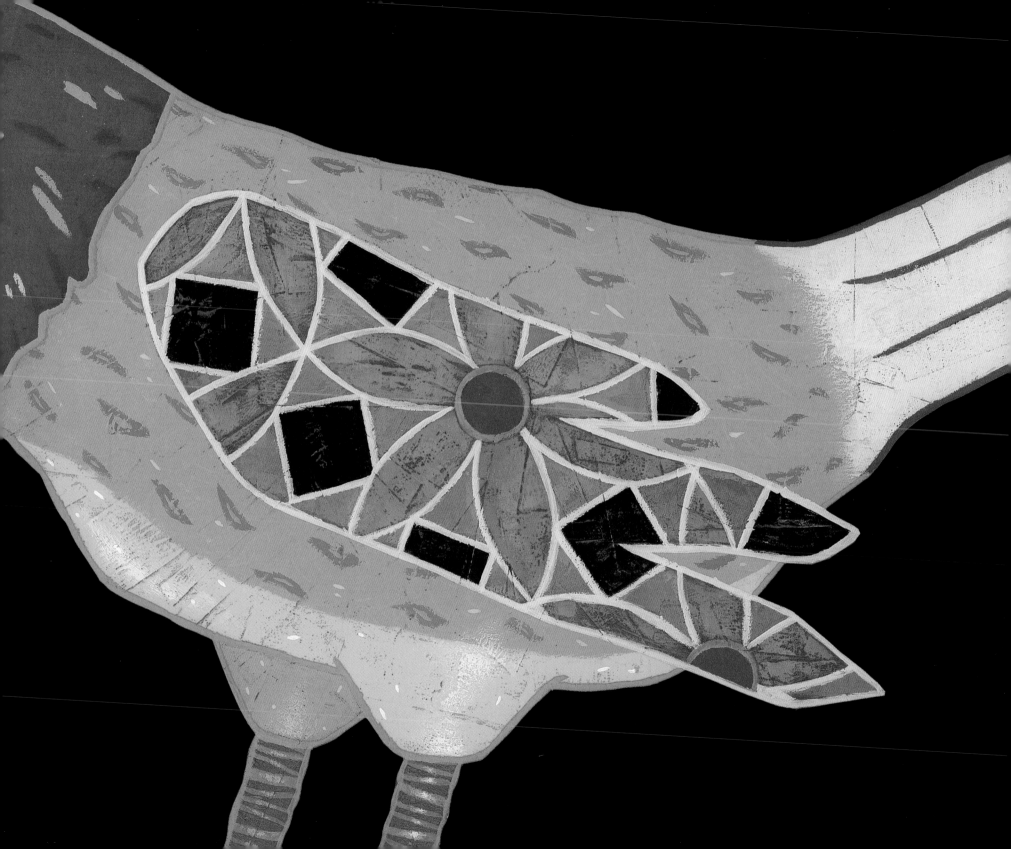

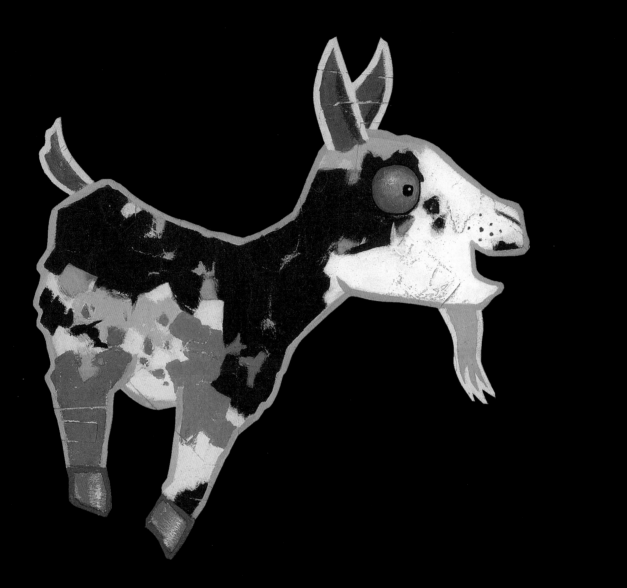

"Now me!" Goat is jumping up and down. "Now me! Now me!"

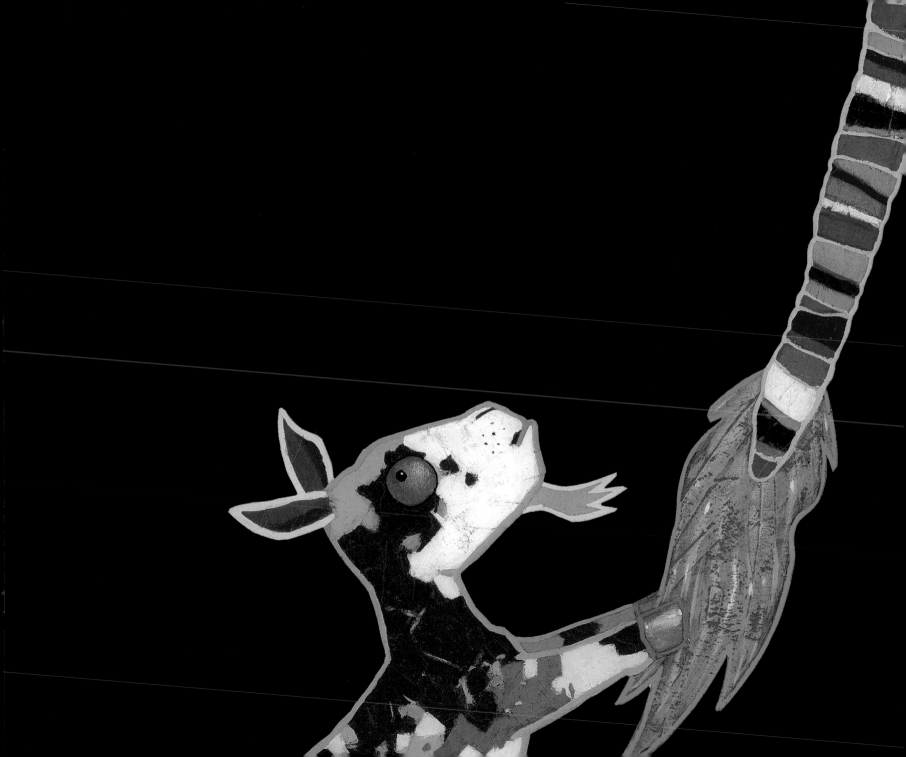

"Ah-ha," snorts Goat. "That's no bird! I felt a goatee. Just like **my** goatee— but fantastically, amazingly extra superduper big. A fantastically, amazingly extra superduper big goat is rustling out there."

"What **is** rustling out there, anyway?" whispers Bat.
"I've got it," whispers Goat. "Listen, this is serious.
What we have here is a whopper of a Tur-Bat-Octo-Bird-Goat!"

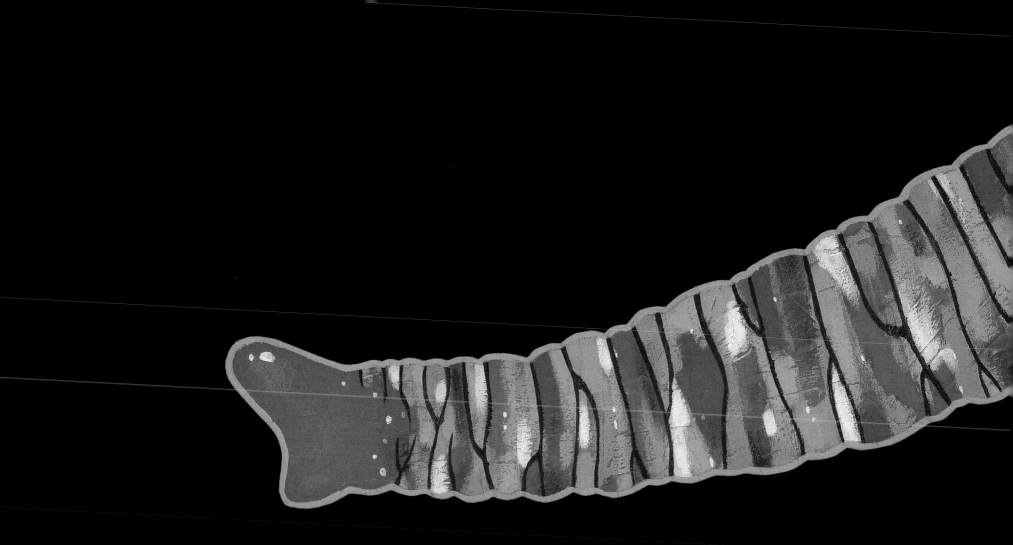

Suddenly there's a tremendous bellow, as if a brass band
were about to play.
"Ha! Ha!" someone trumpets. "A Tur-Bat-Octo-Bird-Goat!
No such thing around here! I'm just an ordinary ..."

"Elephant!"

they all shout together.

"I couldn't sleep," Elephant says.
"The night was too quiet
until you came.
   "That turtle foot was my foot," he says,
lifting one leg. "That bat
wing was my ear. That
tentacle was my trunk.
That beak was my tusk.
And that goatee ..."
Elephant gives another trumpeting laugh.
"That goatee was the tuft of my tail!"

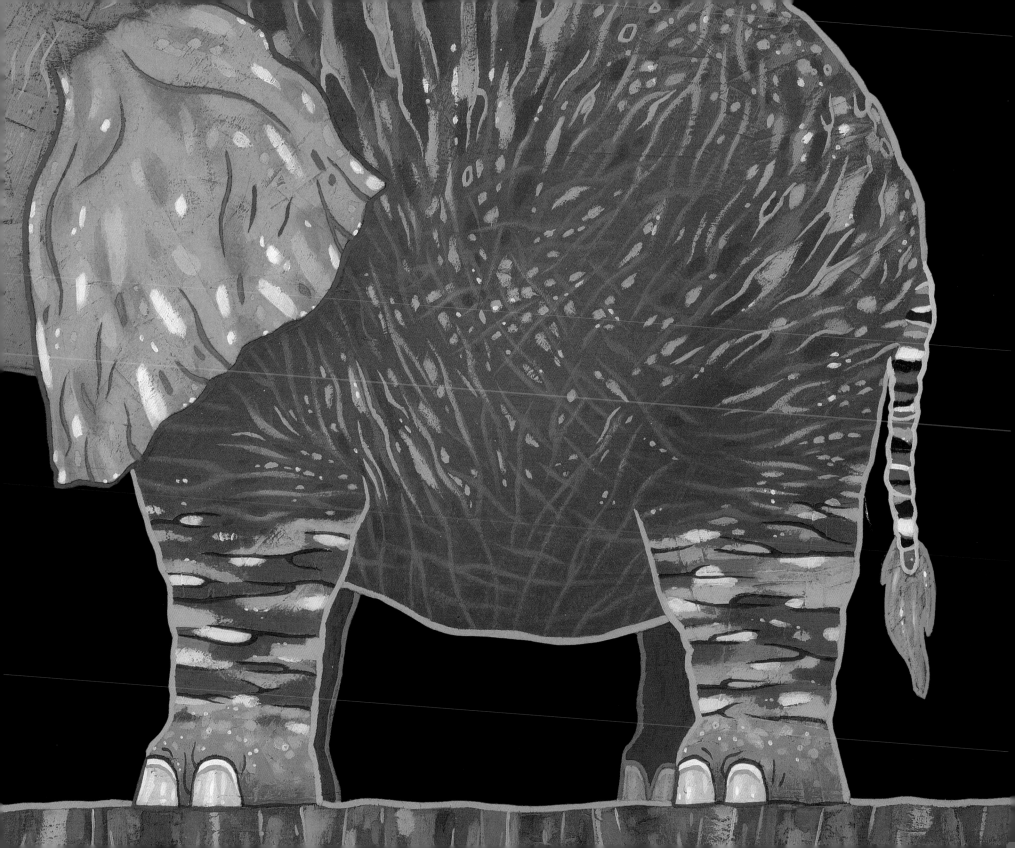

Everybody laughs. Elephant bows his head.
"I am sorry I scared you," he says.
   "Doesn't matter," says Bat.
   "It was a little creepy," giggles Bird.
   "Not for me," says Goat. "I knew what it was all along."
   Octopus yawns. "Let's go back to our hammock."
   "Oh," says Elephant, a little downcast.
   "Elephant," asks Turtle, "would you like to ...?"

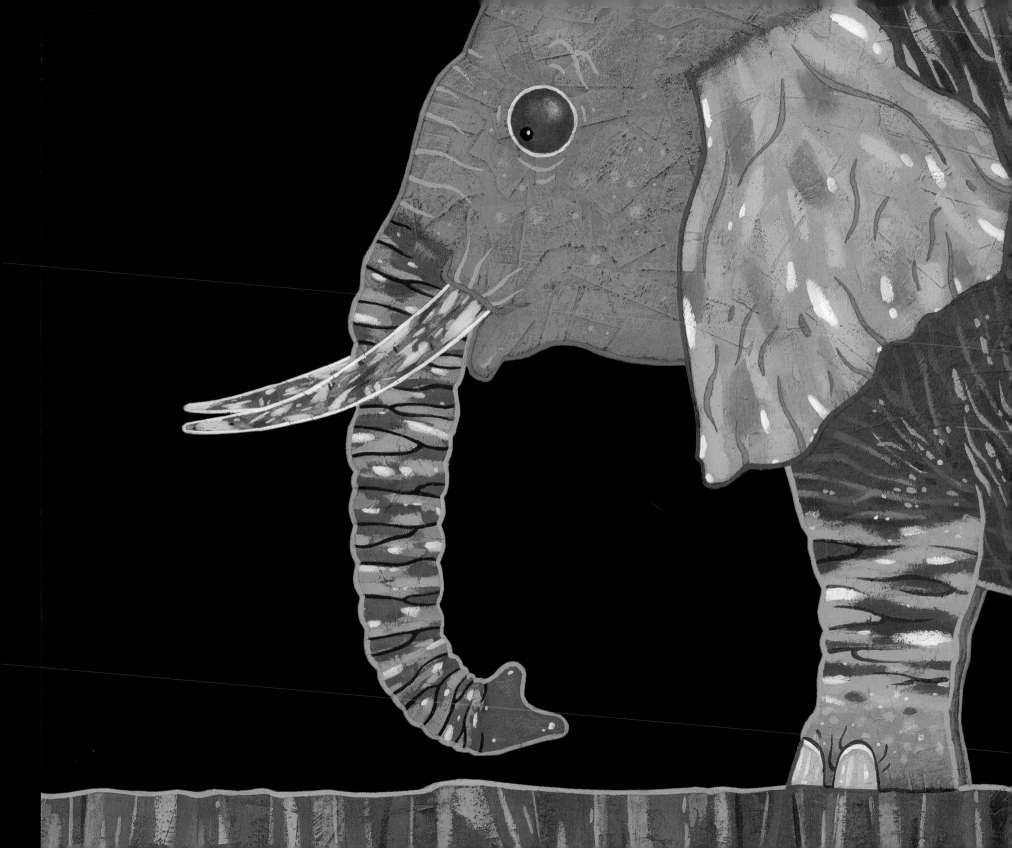

Between two trees, hanging just above the grass, Turtle, Bat, Octopus, Bird, Goat, and Elephant are asleep in their hammock.

Suddenly Elephant opens his eyes. "Hey," he whispers, "do you hear what I hear?"